The Shunt

A Horror Novella

SEAN DEMPSEY

ISBN: 9798339942030

DEDICATION

I dedicate this dreadful novella to my wife, who is a far better and more noble creature than the rough facsimile I portray in these pages.

I also dedicated this story to my beautiful, strong-willed daughter. May she one day *listen* to her Daddy…

ACKNOWLEDGMENTS

NB: This is a <u>derivative</u> work.

What follows is my very first attempt writing in a genre for which I have no right to even pretend comprehension. I give full credit where all credit is due. This work was STRONGLY influenced by the great *Stephen King*. And while every word of this novella is my own, the original concept belongs to the dark and beautiful mind of King—in whose mighty shadow I remain but a simpleton.

A forever and ever (and ever) humble fan,

Sean M. Dempsey

TABLE OF CONTENTS

CHAPTER 1

"But I don't wannnnnna go!" whined a twelve-year-old blonde girl from the backseat as the car sped down the *M406* Motorway. "*Please* don't make me."

"Ava, please try to settle down," her father said slowly and deliberately, trying hard not to lose his temper. "You know this trip has been planned for months now. We've talked about it. We've talked it to death. We are literally on our way. You're a big girl; you have to accept this is happening…"

"Mummy, please," replied Ava, crossing her arms and pouting. "Tell Dad to turn around."

"Sweetie," replied her mother—with a far more patient voice than her husband's— "sweetie, as we talked about, once we get to New Guinea, we are going to do a TON of exploring—just you and me. We're going to go sightseeing. We're going to get pizza and check out that cute little café we found on *Musk Maps* which is just around the corner of our hotel. It's going to be great!"

Kayla's voice was soothing, as it always was. It seemed to do the trick because without even a word of affirmation, Ava put her headphones back on and was quiet. The entire family in tow, the black Tesla continued to navigate towards London. At forty-four years old, the driver, Professor Sean Dempsey, was still rather striking despite his age. He boasted quite a bit more salt than pepper in his beard, but it didn't yet reach the top of his head. He reached over and put his left hand on his wife's knee as the car swerved between traffic with little attention needed from him.

"Thanks for that," his eyes glancing towards their daughter behind them. "You nervous for *the Shunt?*" he asked gently.

Kayla shifted in her seat before replying. "No. I mean – not really. Not nervous; just anxious I suppose. I know you take it all the time. So, I know it's safe. It's just a weird feeling as a mother. The 'protection mode' bells are going off and I can't exactly explain it." She sighed and laughed gently. "But ignore all that. I'm glad to finally be going on holiday. It's going to be good for us. Good for our family!" She reached over and kissed her husband on the cheek. "Plus, this place you booked looks amazing! With all the hours you've been putting in on your new book, I feel I haven't really seen you in months." Sean sheepishly smiled and attempted to change the subject. "I read they hand you a pre-made pina colada the moment you step into the lobby. Oh, and they—"

"What time are we going to be there?" Ava loudly interjected with little regard for their conversation. Her headphones were off her head again.

"Get where, sweetie?" her mother replied with an upbeat tone. "To the *LSA* or to Australia?"

"Both, I guess," said Ava restlessly. "I'm bored. And *hungry.*"

"We should be at the *London Shunt Authority* in less than half an hour," replied her father. "And then, depending on how precheck and Injections go, we'll be in New Guinea within two and a half hours after that. We'll be on the beach within three hours, scout's honor." He lifted up his hand by way of providing a solemn promise.

"And you'll let me actually try a real margarita like you promised?" Ava said, leaning forward and peeking her head in between the middle of the two front seats, "Not just a virgin one like before…?"

"Honey, you didn't tell her that, did you—!?" gasped Kayla in mock disbelief. She had already had this conversation with her husband the day before. But she wanted to put on a good show.

"Ah, I'm afraid I did. And a promise is a promise." He leaned to his left and kissed his daughter's protruding head on the cheek. "Yes, sweetie-pie – I'm always as good as my word. You'll have a *real* margarita. But just one. And we'll be going LIGHT on the tequila."

"Okay, deal. I'm beginning to feel better about this trip already," she laughed and eased herself back to sitting position.

"Thank the Lord," said her mother sarcastically.

"But I still am *not* taking a shot. I don't care what you say. I told you before and I'll tell you again. Nope. Nope. Nope." Ava leaned back in her seat and crossed her arms again.

"Oh my God, Kayla. Please speak to her. If this turns into a thing, I swear I'm going to lose it. If we have to pay extra for the knockout gas, I am seriously going to kill her."

A car pulled in front of them a bit too suddenly; the automatic steering made a loud beep and slowed down rather abruptly. It did little to improve Sean's mood. "I wish this thing had automatic honking. *You freakin' idiot!*" he yelled loudly at the driver who couldn't possibly hear him.

"Sweetie," Kayla spoke pleasantly to the backseat, "how

many times do we need to go over this? You know the rules. You have to take an injection before *the Shunt*. That's just how it is. No exceptions."

"But WHHYYYY...?" moaned Ava. "I hate shots. I *hate* them. You know that. Ever since ever and ever I hate them. And no, the rubbing thing doctors sometimes use doesn't make it any better. It always hurts. Why do I have to? Daddy, please tell me why. Can't I just *Shunt* there without it?"

"ABSOLUTELY NOT!" screamed her father—rather abruptly and far more angrily than he intended. His wife glared at him. He immediately corrected his tone and looked back at Ava, who was starting to collect tears in her eyes. "Sweetie, I'm so sorry. I didn't mean to yell."

It didn't help. Ava began to cry.

"Great, just great," his wife hissed. "Good job, honey. *Really* soothing all our nerves here."

Sean leaned back in his chair, removed his glasses, closed his eyes for a moment, and just let the car drive them towards the LSA. The sound of muffled sobs wheezed from behind him.

CHAPTER 2

Arriving at the *London Shunt Authority* some twenty-five minutes later, things were mildly improved. Ava had calmed down after a number of apologies and attempts to reconcile. This was a well-known cycle for Sean and his daughter. He knew their relationship was beautiful, but admittedly tenuous. She was strong-willed. So was he. That's probably why they got along so well; but it also explained why they argued so easily. Yet, apologies always came quick for both sides, and forgiveness did too.

"We're here." said Sean, letting the car park itself in the massive 12-story parking garage.

"Finally!" sighed Ava with undue exasperation. The trip had only taken around an hour from their home in Epping.

They grabbed their bags from the backseat and trunk, then worked their way to the elevator. Walking in, Sean pressed the button marked "*Shunt Terminal #16*"—which matched their tickets. They shared the elevator with a man in his mid-sixties, dressed in overalls and smelling strongly of cashews. The metallic box started to move with a groan.

"I'm still not taking a *shottttttta*…." Ava's voice hummed

whimsically off-tune, seeking to strike a nerve.

"Yes, you *arrreeee*," hummed her mother in the same musical language under her breath.

Sean just grumbled and pretended not to be bothered by his daughter's attempt to goad him. The elevator doors opened into a wide, massive room. It was floor-to-ceiling *white*, and the external windows looked out on lush, vibrant gardens. Sean had been here many times, so it was a familiar sight. But Kayla gasped, and Ava even stopped humming.

"Wow. This is *beautiful*," whispered Ava in a trance, exiting the elevator and staring forward. The central area had people seated all around on white chairs and vendors quietly conducted business with an air of reserved dedication. Quiet classical music tinged the eardrums as vendors handed out drinks.

"Very *zen*," remarked her mother.

"Yes, it is nice. I agree," said Sean. "It's supposed to be rather peaceful. At least I think it is."

A man dressed in a tan suit and riding in a golfcart-like vehicle approached them nearly immediately. "May I bring you to your assigned seats, folks?"

"Why, of course you can, my good sir," Sean spoke pleasantly. He knew it was not a request, but a well-hidden directive; the LSA did not approve of wandering and ensured all guests got right to their seats for processing. But the luxury service illusion worked its magic, and the girls were impressed.

"Would you like to stop for a smoothie before going to your seats?" asked the man in tan.

"Oh, that sounds great. Daddy, *please*, can we?" Ava made a face that crumpled her lips on each other and gave him puppy-dog eyes. It was a look he could never resist.

"Sure, why not?" replied her father, "Let the vacation *begin*!"

The mood was improving, and nerves were becoming less frazzled. What better way to help lubricate a stressful experience than a fruit smoothie?

After choosing their desired fruits and paying roughly fourteen times more than they would elsewhere (much to Sean's well-vocalized chagrin), the family received their drinks and were ushered to their seats. A large clock on the white wall read 12:26PM. They had just over two hours until their *Shunt*. Since they were so early, they had this section all to themselves. They sat down and began to eat. In between slurps, Ava looked at her father and sighed, "Daddy, I'm sorry. You know I love you. But I still really, really, *really* don't want to take a shot. They hurt! Why do I need to take one?"

The sugar-rush helped, and Sean could better hold his composure than earlier. "You know perfectly well why, sweetie. ***Because I say so!*** " he grinned to show he spoke in good humor, "Plus, I'm sure you've read all about *Shunting* in school. What more do you need to know?"

Gentle music was in the air, emanating from speakers shaped like tall grass in the raised garden by the nearby window. The tune was like something you'd hear in a spa. The family was seated at the very end of the last aisle. Sean had picked these seats intentionally, as they likely would be the last ones to be *Shunted*.

"Well, I guess – like, could you explain *why* we need to be asleep? And, like, how exactly does *the Shunt* even really work? Some kids at school say it's *dark magic* and we'd see **devils** if we were *Shunted* while awake. The teachers are too busy dealing with all the overly-medicated kids to teach us anything really worthwhile. So, like – I don't know. Can you explain it?"

Sean took off his glasses and wiped the lenses with his shirt. He smiled, "Of course I can, sweetie. In fact, I can probably explain it better than most. You do know my entire new book is on the *Shunt Process*, its history, and its many secrets?"

"Yea...um. Actually, I didn't know that at all," she laughed awkwardly. "You've been so busy writing that I didn't even know what you're writing about these last few months. This is the most I've even seen you in like weeks..." Ava's voice trailed off melancholy while she looked at her dangling feet.

Kayla shifted in her seat a bit and put her arm around her daughter. "But we're proud of Professor Daddy for working so hard, aren't we?"

"Of course, Mum."

Sean considered momentarily if there was enough time to go through the whole story. Probably not, but an abbreviated version might help sooth nerves. As a scientist, he understood that demystifying the unknown can often serve as a catalyst to relax unjustified concerns. *The Shunt* was all just Science, after all!

"Well, okay then. I'll explain the history of *the Shunt*. At least, I will on two very important conditions—"

Ava looked excited. "What's that?"

"One: you have to call me '*Doctor Daddy*' while I explain things." Ava rolled her eyes.

"Yea, yea, yea... And?"

"And you have to promise to pay close attention. No getting distracted. I'll only **teach** if you actually want **to learn**."

"Deal, Prof Daddy." exclaimed Ava, finishing her smoothie and putting the plastic cup under her seat. "I'm all ears."

"Right on. Ok, then. I'll explain the miraculous and storied history of *the Shunt*…"

CHAPTER 3

Professor Dempsey quickly assumed his most blustery and professorial voice for narration. He was quite used to speaking in front of large student crowds about his research and various writings, so this seemed like fun practice. He might have to dumb down the language a tad, but that shouldn't be too hard, he reasoned.

"So … the thing you must remember, class, is life was very different fifty years ago—which is approximately when *the Shunt* was invented. It was August 6, 2025…."

"Is that date actually true?" Ava immediately interrupted, looking to her mother for confirmation. She knew her father regularly made-up extraneous details in order to seem extra smart.

"Very true, sweetie. Your dad just finished a very comprehensive book on this exact topic. He knows what he's talking about. About *this* topic at least…" she laughed.

"Anyway, as I was saying…" Sean pretended to sound insulted, then pushed forward using his doctoral voice again, "It was August 6, 2025. As I'm sure even your public school has taught you by now, this was a very dark time, especially for us here in the UK. The start of a vicious *Depression* had just begun; the London Stock Exchange and the US stock markets had both tanked. **Seven** different Asset Bubbles created by the American *Federal Reserve* all burst—and all roughly at the same time! The financial disease quickly spread to the entire world. To add salt to the wounds, oil was spiking throughout the globe —so much so that people like your grandfather had to wait in lines for HOURS to get a little bit of fuel for their vehicles. Back then most cars (and pretty much anything) ran on gasoline…"

"Just say it was 'very bad.'" Kayla spoke up gently, sensing their daughter was already starting to lose focus.

"It was very, *very* bad."

Kayla nodded in accord.

"Ava, it was so bad that people couldn't eat! Many people starved. Only government employees or the super wealthy people had anything at all. And worst of all – the cost of gasoline was so high that many folks (basically anybody who didn't work from home) could barely afford to live. If I remember my notes correctly, it averaged £267.00 per liter for gasoline. And to make matters even WORSE, the *politicians* soon got involved! Not knowing their eh… butt … from their elbows, they decided to put **price controls** in place and blamed 'the evil oil companies' for 'price gouging.' All that did was dry up gasoline completely. Within a month following the idiotic price gouging laws, no one could get gas—no matter how much money they had. Basically, what this meant is that the entire economy was at a standstill!" Sean paused for effect, "Do you know what that means?"

"Yes, I think so. It means no one was making or selling anything, right?"

"Righto," said Professor Dempsey, out of character. His

bravado voice was slipping. "I mean, that's correct, young lady. A+. And please remember to address me as *Doctor Daddy*!"

"Oh, yea, I forgot. Sorry, *Doctor Dad*."

"Anyway, about this point in the story we meet our protagonist. I assume you know what that means…?"

Ava blinked. "…oh, yes, yes. It means like the hero, right?"

"Correct. Our protagonist in August of 2025 is a young scientist named **Doctor Danielle Hastings**. Overworked. Underpaid. But smart. VERY smart. And hell-bent on solving the world's energy crisis…."

Kayla was looking wide-eyed at her husband. The story was kind of engrossing. And he did have a flair for storytelling. She didn't know a lot of this; much of the history of *the Shunt* was hidden from the public. The teachers glossed over this period of history when she went to school. She understood why the kids in her daughter's class thought of it as magic. In fact, she remembered when she was Ava's age her friends all called it *Floo Powder*. She was a big Harry Potter nut back then. But if she was honest with herself, it's how she still thought about it: far more *magic* than science.

Sean continued, "Work was drying up. There was a huge shortage of food worldwide. Inflation devastated the poor and middle-class. It caused prices to soar and made everyone's money almost worthless. On top of all this, the United States was on the verge of war on multiple fronts—and naturally dragging its allies along with it. The US was pressuring NATO to violently force its way eastward, much to the chagrin of Russia. And US President Harris was also vying for war with China and Iran at the same time as bleeding its resources dry by sending massive amounts of newly-printed money to try and prop up Israel. The UK, of course, was following along in its path like a lazy little brother begging for approval. It was a very dark time. But, as your teachers will tell you, the most pressing issue of all was OIL!"

"Oil?" asked Ava.

"Yes, we don't give much thought to it now. But OIL was once called 'liquid gold.' Without oil, crops didn't get planted, and houses didn't get built. Without oil, nothing happened. Due to inflation, many countries completely drained their strategic oil reserves. As a result, gasoline prices spiked; shortly after that, world economies collapsed. That's why oil was at the *heart* of a global crisis in mid-2025."

"Honey? You're losing your audience again."

"Sorry, I mean to say—it was bad! *Very* bad. People were dying. Cats and dogs were living together! Total mayhem."

That got her attention. Ava's eyes sprang open, slightly confused, but fully immersed. She adored all animals.

"Things were horrible. But Dr. Danielle Hastings was the smartest scientist in the world. And guess where she was working?" Sean paused to see if his daughter would know the answer.

"Where?" asked his wife instead, sucked in by the story. Ava looked at her and smiled.

Sean grinned, enjoying the fact his history lesson was being appreciated. "In her *basement!* The smartest scientist in the known world ... was toiling all alone in her basement in Monkton, Maryland – that's over in the United States. I suppose many of the most interesting things get invented in people's garages and basements. And so, too, it was with *the Shunt...*"

****

"*Damn!*"

"Damn, damn, damn." swore Danielle Hastings as she licked her swollen finger and stared down at the machine. This damned machine. Half her professional life had been spent on it. Most of her career was wasted on it.

The transistor assembly was still giving her problems. *Something* was always giving her problems!

It was always the little things. Except, of course, when it was the big things.

If it wasn't the transistors, it was the networked computer core. If it wasn't the core, it was the particle generator module. And, of course, the CODE was constantly being written and re-written to allow for faster and faster processing power to do its magic. But right now, it was the wiring harness in Portal One's main assembly unit. The current on the green B-volt was more than 14db below normal specs. At least she had found the cause fairly quickly: a frayed wire. She fumbled with the repair job clumsily. After a few more minutes she got it sorted.

"Well, *good enough for government work*," she chuckled to herself, believing the fix sufficient enough to attempt another test before her access to the datacenter's Application Programming Interface was limited again in a couple of hours.

She had no choice but to laugh at the sad association of *government work* with her own. When faced with laughing or crying she preferred to laugh. She had never dreamed of becoming caught in the pocket of the *US government*. But desperate times called for desperate measures.

Her private funding had all dried up. Her utility patents had only gotten her so far. And the appetite for non-oil-related or non-food-related scientific grants had gone the way of the dodo. So, she was on her own. Sort of. A last-ditch effort to secure funding landed her on the proverbial doorstep of Washington DC.

She had explained to her contact in Washington the potential uses for her nascent technology. She had even, cautiously, shared some of her initial datasets. And much to her astonishment, the government gave her a $12.25M stipend to continue fueling her research. She had to couch the language of her proposal in bureaucracy and explain the myriad benefits to "national defense" and the "betterment of the American hegemony," *yadda yadda.*

Of course, in the proposal she didn't actually use the word *hegemony*; but the implication was so ripe she could taste it. The sarcasm was lost, however; the US government granted her 100% of the funding she needed to proceed. The deal with the devil was made.

But the money was *just enough.* It was enough for the remaining lab equipment she needed. It was enough for the computer processing interface she required. It was enough for the hardware and the software. It just wasn't enough for an honest-to-goodness workspace.

So here in her basement she languished.

All the better. It was quiet down here, and the hours flew by without interruptions. Good luck getting that in some university or government laboratory!

The computer beeped. Her compile was complete. She ran over to it. The results looked good. But they looked good last time. She sighed. Better try another test.

She pressed buttons on her computer, signaling for another call to roughly 151 APIs she had tied into the AI sequencing algorithm at the government's supercomputer cloud-based datacenter.

She knew every one of these little tests cost hundreds of dollars! But at this point she was getting desperate. She had to be close. If she willed it hard enough, she had to be able to manifest it. All the data looked good. *Why wasn't it working?*

She walked back over to Portal One. She looked up and again analyzed the full hardware setup across her basement lab. Just as she had done eighteen-thousand times before…

Standing at the nucleus of her lab, she stood directly in front of Portal One. It was the exact same 6.25" x 6.25" specifications listed on the official patent she had on file with the US Patent Office. The device buzzed and hummed with electricity connected to the particle converters. They were set up like vertical and horizonal posts—positioned on four equidistant sides of an open square with a hole in the middle. In fact, she now affectionally just referred to Portal One as the "*Square Donut*" because it was basically just a wide hole with the converter assembly (and hundreds of electric wires) carefully positioned around it.

That's a lie, though. It wasn't always an *affectionate* term she used. If pressed, Danielle could probably think of at least twenty times just this week alone she had called Portal One "the bitch donut, " "the damned donut," "the cursed donut," or even far worse labels she wouldn't dare repeat in polite company. But as she stood next to Portal One, the *Square Donut*, she looked across the room.

There on the other side was Portal Two, precisely 12.5 meters away. It was perched atop twelve thick physics books for support. She had measured the height of the portal exactly—to account for any variability. The two portals stood directly across from each other. She had even used lasers to ensure the distance and height were exact—at least to within

$1/100^{th}$ of a millimeter. She walked over to Portal Two. It never received a cute moniker like Portal One, even though they looked literally identical. She just didn't have the same kinship with it. She didn't know why. Maybe she didn't make it over here as often. Portal One was nearer to her computer station, where she spent 98% of her day.

But the hardware was all rather superficial to be honest. The hardware was the "easy" part. All the important stuff happened in the code. The Code. The code was where the breakthrough would come. The code was where the *magic* happened!

CHAPTER 4

Danielle had witnessed the magic once before. And it really was like magic. Most certainly it happened by accident, but it was what kept her moving forward. She had SEEN it with her own eyes. A *Shunt* effect happened right in front of her. She was working on re-wiring one of the transistors on the *Square Donut* just fourteen months ago while the code was recompiling.

Unbeknownst to her, the code finished just as she put her finger around the edge to flick off a loose copper wire hair that had fallen onto the bottom section of the *Donut*. She had moved to pick up (or flick off, she couldn't recall) the loose copper hair. But when she did so, her front index finger and part of her thumb vanished! *Completely vanished*! She pulled back her hand so violently she knocked the entire *Donut* assembly on the ground; parts broke off and went everywhere.

She remembered expecting to see blood. In fact, her mind *tricked* her – making her actually SEE blood squirting out of her fingers. But upon a second look, the fingers were fine. She got them out of her mouth (an instinctual reaction) and looked at them. They were perfectly whole. She wiggled her hand and moved each finger up and down repeatedly. There wasn't a scratch on them!

That was *fourteen* months ago. At times she wondered if she had imagined the whole thing.

It took three months to repair the damaged equipment. And many more months than that to try to replicate the experiment. The compiled code she had been using at the time also seemed to have been woefully insufficient to handle the full data load of the 'experiment'; it threw hundreds of exceptions and programming faults which she had spent weeks trying to decipher and vigorously document. She felt lucky to still have her fingers given the subpar quality of her poorly written code!

But she had done it. Briefly, if not accidentally, she had proved that *Shunting* worked. And if she was to be believed (and was to believe her own eyes), she HAD to get it working again!

Danielle walked back to her computer terminal and looked down at her watch. 3:43pm. She had less than an hour and a half of use of the government's cloud computing network. Luckily the compiling was just finishing up.

Chirp! *Chirpy. Chirp, Chirp.*

The computer loudly played an .mp3 file of sparrows singing. Not long ago, she had set up this basic 'warning system' to let her know exactly when a code-compiling cycle was complete. Good science didn't need to always be sterile, she figured. Testing could now commence.

She returned to the table holding the *Square Donut*. Cautiously, she pushed her test ping-pong ball through the hole…

****

"*Professor Daddy*—" Ava had her hand up in the air, mocking the presentation of the story.

"Yes, yes, you there! The young lady in the green shirt in the front row? Can I help you?"

"Why did Dr. Danielle use a ping-pong ball?"

"What? —of all the questions you might have...that's what you're curious about?"

Ava looked slightly embarrassed. "Professor Daddy, I withdraw the question."

"Haha, no it's okay. I honestly have no idea, sweetie. What I do know is that the ping pong ball came on loan to *The British Museum* just last year. It now sits behind about ten centimeters of glass and is protected with 24-hour video surveillance. It was the first item ever to be *Shunted* in human history!"

Her mum spoke up excitedly, "Actually, Ava, I think you'll be pleased to know that your class will be going there first thing next year. *Shunt World Celebration Month* is in August as you know; and your eighth-grade class next year will be doing a field trip to London at the start of the school year! So, you'll get to see the exact ping-pong ball Doctor Hastings used! Won't that be exciting!?"

Ava looked at her mother and blinked. "Um... no. So, I'll get to go see a ping pong ball? Great."

Kayla's voice fell flat, mildly dejected. "Just keep listening to your father...."

Professor Dempsey smiled and looked at his watch. They still had at least another hour and a half until their designated *Shunt* time. "Ok, well, anyway, where was I? Oh, yes – so the ping-pong ball..."

****

Dr. Hastings pushed the ping-pong ball ever so gently through the Portal...

And then – it was gone.

Just *GONE*!

On the other side of the room, Danielle heard it. She looked up immediately. There was the ping-pong ball bouncing up and down on the floor – right underneath Portal Two.

CHAPTER 5

"Oh my God. Oh my God. Oh my God. Oh my God." Danielle muttered under her breath as she stared at the bouncing ball.

It had worked.

She stared in disbelief. Her legs refused to even move. All the years of hard work – all the sleepless nights, all her desperate pursuit of a single goal, all the sacrifice and struggle – it all seemed like a dream. She stared at the bouncing ball and started to laugh involuntarily. It was an unconscious, almost delusional laugh. Alone in the dim basement, surrounded only by buzzing hardware and papers strewn about on desks, she laughed and crazily watched a ping-pong ball bounce across the floor of her makeshift lab.

It finally stopped bouncing and she was left only with the sound of gentle humming from the *Donut* directly below her. Finally, after what seemed like forever, she was able to will her muscles to move. She walked – then ran – across the room to Portal Two. The ball had rolled a few feet away; she picked it up.

Danielle stared at it. It looked whole. It looked no different.

Grabbing it in her hands, she ran back to Portal One. With reckless abandon and no thought of taking notes or logging scientific data on the phenomenon, she threw the ball through the Portal – then immediately looked up to examine Portal Two across the room. Immediately the ball emerged from it and went spinning and bouncing into the corner.

It worked!

There appeared to be no discernable lag or delay. Up until now, that was her biggest fear. The impact on molecular cohesion which could be caused by even a fraction of a millisecond delay in the particle diffusion would be incalculable based on her projections. But there was none. *The Shunt* was virtually seamless.

She ran to the corner, leaned over, and picked up the ping pong ball. Peering at it again, she could see no discernable changes in the object; its cohesion appeared flawless to the naked eye. The hand-drawn lines she had previously made around the ball, tracing three separate circumferences using a felt-tipped pen, were fully preserved. Not a single spot looked out of place. Putting the ball away, she hurried over to her computer desk and hungrily gazed for another object in which to test her invention.

She grabbed a *G2 Premium Gel Roller Pen* lying atop a stack of papers and turned back to her device. The *Square Donut* buzzed back at her as she approached. She was almost giddy with excitement.

Getting down to eyeball level with the Portal, Danielle slowly placed the pen into the *Donut* hole. As it moved, the pen started disappearing while she held onto it. She could see the front of the pen get smaller and smaller as she pushed it through the portal.

She then had an idea. She stopped pushing and let the

bottom half of the pen rest on the lower lip of the *Donut*. The bottom of the pen looked like it was defying gravity, as there was not enough mass showing to possibly counterbalance its weight as it lay there. She looked up across the room and could see the front of the pen sticking out on the other side. She let go of it and walked over to Portal Two.

Looking down and gazing at the situation from multiple angles was astounding. The front of the pen was there - sticking out from the Portal. When looked at from the back of the portal, the pen seemed divided in half, like a sandwich cut down the middle—or, more accurately, like a severed tree trunk being looked at from the top.

She could clearly see the black ink, and the mechanical plastic elements of the pen around it. But the pen was not leaking fluid. It simply looked sliced in half, cauterized by some strange process, and stuck in space.

After multiple minutes of walking around and staring at the pen, she grabbed the front of it and pulled it through.

The pen was fine. It was in perfect working condition.

She clicked the 'clicky part' on the end of it a few times, to be sure. Everything worked; the front tip came out and retracted again. She ran back to her computer desk. Grabbing a piece of paper only-half filled with hand-scribbled notes, she brought the pen down and quickly wrote:

THE SHUNT WORKS!

She looked back at her watch again. 4:41pm.

No! She only had nineteen minutes left before her access to the AI-powered supercomputer network was suspended until tomorrow morning. She had to get busy.

She didn't miss a moment. Danielle spent the next eleven minutes quickly setting up ad hoc recording equipment, sensors, distance-measuring lasers, and a handful of other testing tools. For the remaining eight minutes she sent three pieces of paper, two additional pens, her watch, a double-A battery, and finally her iPhone through the portal.

She carefully documented her findings for each test and recorded each *Shunt* attempt using a video camera placed haphazardly on her computer desk.

At 4:59pm, following her last test – *Shunting* her *iPhone 16 Max* as the first high-tech guinea-pig – she pulled it gingerly from the lip on the bottom of Portal Two and clicked the green *Phone* icon on the screen. It worked without the slightest hiccup. She pressed the *Favorites* star icon at the bottom of the screen, then clicked the name she wanted and went to speaker.

When a voice finally answered, Danielle screamed into the phone—her eyes streaming with elated tears:

"Mom … *EUREKA. EUREKA*!!"

CHAPTER 6

"They're all there you know?" said Kayla excitedly to Ava while she stared at her father speaking.

"Huh? Who's there?" asked Ava, turning to look at her mother sitting beside her.

"The pen. The paper. The battery. Even a toothpick. You forgot to mention the *toothpick*, honey!"

"Ah, indeed I did. Thank you for correcting me." Sean looked down at Ava and smiled. "I forgot the toothpick."

"The toothpick is where? What are you talking about?" said Ava, confused.

"In The British Museum, of course." said her mother excitedly. "They're all there—right next to the ping-pong ball. It's a fun exhibit. You're going to love it."

"Oh. My. God. Seriously, you guys. I can't tell if you're messing with me. Who cares about a *toothpick* or a ping-pong ball? What happened next, Dad?"

"*Doctor Daddy,* I believe you mean, little girl—"

"Ugh. Yes, Professor Dad. Yes, sir, what happened next?

Did Dr. Danielle save humanity, I assume?"

Sean paused. "Uh—well, yes. Of course, ultimately, she did. But not right away. Next came some more tests of course. Us doctors and scientists do love our tests, you know…"

****

After a brief and excited call with her mother, Dr. Danielle Hastings was exhausted. She looked around the cluttered basement, which somehow looked quite different. Bigger. The couch where she often passed out after 18–20-hour days was there in the corner. It used to depress her to see the disorderly condition of her "lab," but today she felt positively giddy. She felt beyond giddy. She felt like she could fly!

She immersed herself in data collection. With the two Portals reduced to nothing more than paperweights until 5:00am tomorrow when the connection to the government supercomputers was restored, she used the next hour to examine the items she had *Shunted*. Although it wasn't the first item she sent through, for convenience she put the pen under a high-powered microscope to examine it for any glaring issues or items of concern. After nearly twenty minutes of detailed observation, she could find not a single molecule out of place.

Dr. Hastings did admit to herself, and described in her notes, that there was a glaring lack of viable *baselines* with respect to her findings. She kicked herself for not having taken x-ray imaging scans, microscope imagery—nor even basic photographs—of the objects such as the ping pong ball and the pen prior to *Shunting* them.

Establishing baseline data was crucial. If she was going to publish her research, she would look like a piss-poor scientist for not having the good sense to do baseline analysis. But there was plenty of time for that tomorrow.

THE SHUNT ✦ SEAN DEMPSEY

She detailed her findings in a hand-written journal, then completed a video log formally wrapping up the day's progress and next steps. She turned off the video camera and looked at her watch – 6:33pm.

There was so much more data to collect before she even could think of calling her government handlers. She walked over to her computer and pulled up the *Musk Search Engine*. She typed in a query and got the answer she needed:

The nearest pet store closed in twenty-seven minutes. *She had time.*

CHAPTER 7

Sean looked up from his story to gaze into his daughter's face. He knew the mention of animals would get her attention. He was right. She looked fascinated.

He considered his narrative approach for a fraction of a second. He had to use this time of rapt attention to elucidate some scientific background—something he knew she hated, or at least pretended to hate in order to bother him.

"Now to just briefly pause this delicious history lesson for a quick scientific breakdown of the *Shunting Process*," he began in his best professorial voice.

"Oh, God, no please," his daughter squirmed in her seat.

"Tut, tut. I know you'll love being the smartest girl in class soon. For what kind of father would I be if I didn't share just a brief word about particle transference. AKA 'the magic of *the Shunt*.'"

"Please don't. What's Dr. Danielle going to the pet store for?"

"We'll get to that soon enough, honey. But first – it's

important to understand that for decades prior to this, the typical computer—while still vastly more powerful than the one man even used to go to the moon in the late 1960s—was still basically in the 'stone age' when it came to computing power."

"Got it. Computers sucked long ago. Ok, pet store time…?" Ava crossed her arms.

Her father ignored her. "Contrary to popular opinion, *the Shunt* is NOT magic. Not even close. It's a scientific process. But it is one that only highly sophisticated computers could provide."

Ava pretended to yawn. Sean continued nonetheless, "See, the emergence of AI in 2024 changed the game forever. Allowing AI to interface with networked supercomputers in 'the cloud' unlocked *massive* computing power. These chained networks of AI-powered supercomputers were optimized for maximum processing power and data throughput. *Millions* of processors could work in parallel to solve complex problems and transfer or compile data in a fraction of a millisecond."

"*Borrringgggggg….*"

"Anyway, the reason this is important, is that the 'magic'"—he used air-quotes with two of his fingers—"of *the Shunt* device isn't in particle physics, as many people think. It's actually in the ability to move trillions of bits of data around a network instantaneously. Again, it's not magic; it's SCIENCE that's to thank for *the Shunt*!"

"Cool. That's cool. Science is the best. Got it. Is Dr. Hastings getting a cat to help with her experiments? I don't get it."

Sean sighed. Kayla silently chuckled. She knew it was hopeless to try to intentionally instruct their daughter. Any education imposed almost needed to be "tricked" into her.

Nevertheless, she spoke up to try to help. "Do you know the music you listen to on your phone, honey? It's kind of the same thing; only that's just audio files. But it's all just data being whisked around the net—from the cloud to your phone. Just raw data. Physical objects can also be made into just packets of data as well. A lot MORE data, but it's still just data. And so, it takes a much bigger and faster computer to send all the data. Make sense?"

"Yea, I guess so," Ava spoke slowly. "So, the things sent through the portals just get turned into data streams like my music? And then they can be sent to another portal to be 'listened to' or un-*datafied* or whatever?"

Sean spoke up, bemused, "That's actually not a bad analogy, sweethearts. I need to bring you two along on my next lecture tour. It's crude, but accurate. Yes, just as you said, *the Shunt* Device essentially moves highly complex data that's decoupled from physical matter via particle synthesis along a data stream through a highly reactive and interlaced network and then it is processed and reconstituted by the AI-powered supercomputing meshwork located in the cloud. Make sense?"

Ava blinked.

"Dad…"

"Yes, sweetie?"

"You're a total nerd. You know that right?"

Sean sighed again and continued the story.

****

Doctor Hastings rushed out the door to her vehicle. Given how little gas she had left, she hadn't left her house for over a week.

She started the engine. Only 1/32 gal left in the tank—and that was an optimistic appraisal of the situation. Nevertheless, this was important.

She drove uptown gingerly, trying hard to "ride the gravity" on hills to preserve as much gas as possible. The techniques to preserve critical gasoline were being emailed and texted to citizens every other day by government officials as a safety precaution. Although it was ninety degrees outside, she kept the AC off to preserve fuel (another tip they routinely shared).

She arrived fifteen minutes later and exited her vehicle, sweat beading off her forehead. It was 6:54pm. She ran inside. She knew she probably looked slightly unhinged, but she didn't even care. Running to the middle of the room on the left, she saw what she wanted and flagged an attendant.

"I'll take your entire supply of these. Yes, yes – only four? Fine, well, okay. Yes, all four please."

She soon paid and exited the store with a white *Petco*-branded cardboard box in her hand.

CHAPTER 8

The car got maybe four miles down the road from *Petco* before completely running out of gas. The car sputtered to a stall and then died completely.

She couldn't say she was surprised. She left it on the side of the road. She had passed perhaps eight or nine other deserted cars on her way back home. It was a normal sight to see these days. Gas was so sparse that people abandoned their vehicles and hitch-hiked or walked when the tanks went dry.

"Two-Ton Paperweights," as the tv networks called them, littered the highways and suburban areas. Without the ability to refill the tanks, the only vehicles that had any practical purpose nowadays were all electric. But they were extremely sparse given their high price tag. Even the most basic Tesla or Volkswagen EZ models sold for over $450,000 per vehicle!

If you wanted to go anywhere, you were likely biking or walking. The bus system still ran in big cities, but the cost to ride the bus was astronomical. Only millionaires could afford a simple transit card.

Danielle sighed and started walking. The little creatures in the cardboard box made clumsy noises and scraped against the thin walls, not appreciating the harsher outdoor summer temperatures. Just after midnight she arrived back home. It was dark. She was dirty. She was exhausted.

She placed the moving box of critters on her kitchen table, found some stale bread in her pantry, and threw it in the box. She filled a small bowl with water and placed it into the box as well.   She then showered and slipped into bed. Although physically exhausted, she could not sleep. She was simply too excited. After a few hours of tossing and turning, she got up and went down to the basement lab. She looked at the clock— 2:56am.

Well, might as well start setting up for work. Big day today. *Perhaps the biggest day of my career,* she thought.

Two hours later, the lab looked pretty gosh-darn respectable. The papers on her desks were organized and put away. She located four additional video cameras she had purchased with the government grant and set them up strategically around the room on tripods. She positioned her testing apparatus for barometric pressure and temperature. She found scales to measure weight. She placed decibel meters around Portal Two. She also had her spectrophotometry kit sitting on the table. She was ready.

The clock struck 5:00am. As she had programmed a year earlier, the lighting in the basement automatically went to full illumination.

The Portals began to hum to life. The connection to the super-computer network was activated again. The real testing could commence.

CHAPTER 9

"Doctor Danielle T. Hastings, analytical reporting. *Shunt Trial 1.10*. 5:06am Tuesday August 7, 2025." Danielle spoke confidently into Camera One, which was sitting on a tripod next to her computer setup and facing towards the two Portals. She fed each video recording into her computer simultaneously with the other feeds. She began streaming the recorded video live to her private network.

"I am about to proceed with the *Shunting* of Object denoted '*Alpha 1.0*': a plastic cup filled with 236ml of room temperature water." She held up a cup of water so the camera could see and continued:

"As noted in the log file attached to this recording (see corresponding file *226-J.log*), I have cataloged the precise temperature, volume, acidity, and spectrophonic readings of Object *Alpha 1.0*. I will now proceed with executing a *Shunt*. Stand by."

Man, did she look the part. Donning a full white lab coat (which was completely for show by the way; she hadn't actually put it on when doing real work in over a decade) as well as goggles and latex gloves, she wanted to make a grand debut onto the scientific scene. She somehow knew the world would one day study these videos closer than the JFK assassination footage.

She moved to Portal One with her gloved hand holding the paper cup of water. She felt slightly silly, but the Scientific Method pushes one's personal qualms to the side.

Professional. Poise. She commanded herself to attention. Danielle very gently pushed the cup of water through Portal One.

It disappeared—just as she expected it to!

Her hands trembled slightly as she spoke, looking now at Camera 2 nearest to Portal One. "*Ah, hem. Yes,* as seen, *Object Alpha 1.0* has effectively *Shunted* to the other side of the room via particle transference. I will now go inspect the object at Portal Two."

She walked professionally to Portal Two, daring herself not to sprint as she did yesterday. Reaching Portal Two, the water was sitting there—exactly as expected. She grabbed the cup and examined it. Then she turned to Camera 3, which was standing head-level beside Portal Two. "As you can see, Object *Alpha 1.0* has *Shunted* exactly 12.50 meters from its origin point, Portal One, to the destination point, Portal Two."

She picked up the water and brought it to the examining table she had hurriedly set up at 4:45am that morning. She gazed into Camera 4 sitting on a tripod just beyond the table. "I will now perform another series of tests on the water in the plastic cup and compare them to baseline."

Her voice was starting to get more sturdy. She knew she must have sounded tense earlier; she just hoped no one would doubt her credibility over a bit of stage fright. She quickly ran through the standard tests she had prepped:

- Volume: **236.00mL**
- Water temperature: **25.6422°C**
- Salinity: **92.7ppm**
- PH: **7.6ph**
- Spectrophotometry results: **Shown in *Log 226-K***

Danielle cleared her throat and spoke, looking back into Camera 4, "As you can see by the results shown, as demonstrated via Camera 5, the water's chemical and physical makeup is precisely consistent with the baseline as shown in *Log 226-J*. In layman's terms: there is no discernable change. Not a hair is out of place!"

She coughed awkwardly. That last sentence was likely not needed. She internally grimaced, determined to only speak using the most precise scientific nomenclature. *Less is more*, she admonished herself.

"I will now proceed onward to the next viable test."

She began to walk through the same tests for multiple items she had collected for this purpose. For the next hour and a half, she *Shunted* a beaker of nitrogen, a paperclip, a pen (although not the same one as the day before), a pencil, a stapler, a piece of paper, a piece of wood, an empty glass, and a magnet. The tests involving the magnet took three times the length as the previous ones to demonstrate that the magnetic field manifested absolutely no change pre- and post-*Shunt*.

"The time is 7:52am Tuesday August 7, 2025. I will now proceed forward with *Shunt Trial 10.10* using *Object Delta-6*: a live test subject, *Cricetus cricetus*. Colloquially known as – a hamster."

CHAPTER 10

"Oh. My. Gosh. Daddy!" Ava's eyes were wide.

Sean opened his mouth to speak. But he caught his wife's eye and closed it again. She looked at him imploringly and silently mouthed something he couldn't quite make out, trying to get his attention.

"Eh---yes. Well, now we get to the heart of real scientific progress, honey. Science demands that we explore and test its boundaries. Doctor Hastings needed to see if *the Shunt* worked with living tissue. To do that, she needed a live test animal."

His wife's silent mouthing looked like something he could finally make out. *"Be very careful"* she seemed to be telling him silently. They both knew the big heart their kid had.

"So, what happened? What happened?"

"Well… it could have gone better, I suppose---"

****

Doctor Hastings reached carefully for the box she had hidden just outside the camera's field of vision. She retrieved one of the hamsters and brought him over to the camera. "Say hello, *Delta-6.*"

She smiled, held him up, and waved his little gray paw at the camera.

Ugh, she didn't know if that was very professional. She kicked herself again quietly then returned to a mature and professional posture. "Please refer to Lab Results *Log 331-A* for a full bodily workup on *Delta-6.* While I did not contain the medical or veterinary equipment pertinent to perform a comprehensive compliment of tests, I did conduct the basic readings such as heart rate, weight, and body temperature, and retrieved a blood and stool sample."

She paused for effect as she walked over to Portal One and Camera 2. "I shall now proceed with *Shunt Trial 10.1.*"

She took a deep breath. She knew this was going to be a defining moment in her career. One way or another. She reached down and brought the hamster in front of the *Donut,* then gently let it go.

At this point – the hamster immediately jumped down off the table and ran along the ground. It scurried out of sight and under her couch on the other side of the room.

Danielle turned a dark shade of red but held her composure. Sure, this was the highlight of her professional career. Sure, this video would be seen by millions—perhaps one day *billions*—of people. And sure, her first live test subject had just blatantly escaped. But forever the optimist, she quickly looked at the camera and commented, "A short pause is needed while I obtain a new test subject. Don't worry; we have backups, folks!"

Danielle walked back to the pet store box (which she had accidentally left open and almost lost her entire stock.) She kicked herself again for nervously rushing but then considered the setback serendipitous. If she hadn't lost the first hamster, then the entire lot of them might have gone missing. *A blessing in disguise?*

She grabbed a fresh hamster from the box. There were now only two left in there.

She then spent the next half hour doing the same baseline tests on cute little *Delta-7* as previously conducted on *Delta-6*.

Coming back to the Camera 1, she repeated her spiel. This time she didn't wave the hamster's paw. All business.

Getting down to the heigh of Camera 2, which was directly facing Portal One, she spoke clearly, "I shall now proceed with *Shunt Trial 10.2* using test subject *Delta-7*."

She brought *Delta-7* to the *Donut*, holding him quite a bit more snugly than she had *Delta-6*. The hamster squeaked at the pressure, and bit her in the top of the thumb. Luckily, her hand was gloved, or it might have hurt a lot more than it did. She could tell it was bleeding but maintained her composure. Not wishing to give the little creature any ability to run, she deftly pushed him through the portal.

Contemplating another embarrassment, Danielle rushed over to Portal Two with a less-than-professional jog. She did not want to risk the hamster jumping down the table on the other side of the room. But the effort was unwarranted.

The hamster just sat there on the table. The boisterous creature which had been lively and squirming and had bitten her finger in angst just a moment ago was quite different. He looked shriveled and ... *old*. Insanely old!

She squatted down and looked at his face. His eyes looked black, glassy, and far gone—almost like a doll's eyes. The creature stood there for a moment—staring—staring into space. Staring at nothing.

Then it let out a doleful, painful gasp unlike anything she had ever heard from an animal, rolled over, and *died*.

CHAPTER 11

S ean looked up and saw a cart on wheels coming out from behind a thick red velvet curtain on the other side of the room. He was expecting this. Four LSA government officials in white suits—three male and one female; they were making their *Propofol* rounds. The required *Shunt* injections were being doled out to passengers in the neighboring terminal. They looked to be *Shunting* soon to Siberia? *Why would someone want to go to Siberia?* he mindlessly thought to himself.

"Daddy, what happened to the hamster?" Ava was wide-eyed.

"Honey, did you really have to go into all that? Was I somehow *unclear*—?" his wife was wearing her *frustrated-and-disappointed* face that he hated more than anything.

"I'm sorry, girls. I'm just sharing the truthful history. A good scientist leaves nothing out. A lot of this you'll be learning in school anyway. I just am trying to add some of the details you wouldn't normally get. *Doctor Daddy* spares no relevant information!" he smiled.

His wife wasn't amused.

Ava still had a look of horror on her face. "What happened to the poor hamster, Daddy?"

The cart was just starting to make its way along the first rows of the adjacent terminal. He figured he had at least another hour to tell the rest of the story. He had hoped it would alleviate some of the fears with *the Shunt*. Thinking about and talking through scientific matters had always worked for him. *But I guess this is slightly different,* he mused.

"Well, to answer that takes a bit of explanation, honey. I'll try to explain. You see, Doctor Hastings--"

****

At first Doctor Hastings didn't exactly know what to do or say. She stared at the little hamster that had been full of spit and vinegar only moments before. She took the carcass and brought it to the testing and analysis table. A tad more somber than expected, she looked into Camera 4 and spoke:

"Subject *Delta-7*. Status: *Deceased.*"

She then conducted a perfunctory set of tests:

- o   Mass: identical to baseline.
- o   Body Temperature: decrease of -0.83°C (but she supposed this was to be expected as the creature was now dead).
- o   Cause of Death: ***unknown***.

Unknown, unknown, unknown.

And what was most bizarre was the vile look and deformity of the creature. Its eyes were deranged. They were stiffly set and wide open— they were wild! They looked tormented, if that was possible for a creature so small. And the body appeared withered and as if it had aged a hundred years in a single moment.

Already stiff with *rigor mortis*, its skin was pasty and felt hard to the touch. The hair on its body, previously brownish red—now looked white. And as she examined the creature, its hair came off in clumps in her hand.

In short, the hamster was now a withered, wild and deranged *demon*. It seemed unnatural. It repulsed her … especially its eyes. Its bloodless, glassy eyes were ghastly. She couldn't bear to look at them. Gathering her composure as best she could, she said, "I am now placing the specimen in a sealed bag for further study and an autopsy at a later date." She turned and paused the recording on all five cameras using a remote control. Then she went and sat down on her sofa bed. The event had traumatized her immensely.

She liked animals as much as the next gal, but this was different. She had been part of hundreds of animal autopsies in her scientific career—hell, in college biology classes alone she had personally dissected nearly fifteen different animals, from a fetal pig to an American bullfrog. She even dissected a cat once in grad school.

But this was different. That hamster looked other-worldly. It looked twisted. *And those glassy, dark, and shallow eyes…*

She didn't know how, but *those eyes* – those eyes had seen pain and torment. There was a dismal, eerie sense of foreboding that came over her.

She walked to the small sink in the far corner of the room and poured a glass of water. She then gained her composure and returned to her desk.

The computer had already collected 321 *terabytes* of information about the preceding 10 *Shunts*. This data would prove invaluable to her research. She paused and considered the future—something she hadn't had a chance to do until now. Yes, if it wasn't possible to transport organic matter that would be a gigantic disappointment. Truth be told, it was the sole reason she worked on this project for as long and as hard as she had these many years.

Yet, she took a moment to ponder all angles. If she could solve the transportation hurdles of moving physical items across large geographic regions then much of the oil consumption catastrophe could be solved virtually overnight. No more trucking convoys; no more cargo planes. No more large vessels moving billions of consumer goods over the ocean. No more freight trains or risky ocean liners spilling precious oil. If particle diffusion and transference could solve these problems, it would still be a revolutionary discovery for humanity. She might one day be held with the same reverence as Alexander Graham Bell or Isacc Newton.

Yet, the organic transfer problem gnawed at her, seeding her with a dark spirit. The thought of getting this far only to lose the race right at the finish line irked her to no end! *To fail when I've gotten this close…*

Danielle, what are you doing? she mused to herself. *You're already claiming defeat before the game has even started!* In fact, if she thought about it, her initial testing had only just begun. There was so much time to figure out this new problem.

However, the devilish eyes of that dead rodent ate at her soul. Despite this, she mustered up all her grit and got back to her feet.

Walking over to the *Petco* box, she grabbed another hamster.

CHAPTER 12

The government attendants were still doing their rounds at the adjacent terminal. Sean could see the passengers squirming in their chairs as they spoke to the attendants. You could always tell the newbies to *the Shunt* by the conversations.

They attempted to hide their nervousness. They would request literature on the drug they were being given (even though they'd doubtlessly read it all before). *They were given a brochure.* They would ask about the drug's efficacy and if it was 100% foolproof (*yes, it was*). The newbies would often nervously ask silly questions about the *Shunting Process* and its etymology or history (*they'd be directed to the brochure*).

These were all just delaying tactics.

The officials had seen it all before a hundred times. They were trained to be patient. Never to force someone to take the injection if they don't want to. Never to argue with a passenger if they become aggressive or overly restless. Just maintain poise and be professional—sterile government efficacy to a tee.

A male official on the far end of the corridor was helping a young lady in her early twenties with her shot. She seemed familiar with the process. Within seconds of receiving the injection, the woman passed out. Her skirt rode up slightly as she slumped in her seat. The LSA agent looked around awkwardly and pretended to help push the skirt back down. While doing so, he got a hand up between her legs and smiled. He looked around furtively and then strapped the woman more firmly into her *Shunt* Passenger Seat. He then proceeded to the next passenger who was a row away. *Typical behavior*, Sean bemoaned silently. But what could you do? The government unions were iron clad; the incident wasn't even worth reporting.

Plus, time was running out. They'd arrive at their terminal soon enough to walkthrough the pre-*Shunt* checklist.

"Dad, what was wrong with the hamster?"

"Well, honey—like I was saying—it's a bit complicated. It's all scientific, of course. See---"

****

Dr. Hastings flipped the cameras back to record and steeled her nerves.

"I am now proceeding with *Shunt Trial 11.1*. Live test subject is again *Cricetus cricetus*. Designation: *Delta-8*."

She moved toward Portal One. Before turning the cameras back on, she had erected a crude makeshift device for the test— a large plastic funnel was positioned halfway through Portal One and halfway out of it. She could see the narrow end emerging across the room at Portal Two. She had placed large physics books on either side of the funnel to give it rigidity and stability.

She placed the hamster inside the funnel. It was too steep a climb at the top to get out. The only way was down—through the tunnel. It was essentially a little makeshift *hamster-slide*.

Faced with a lack of mobility options, the creature sniffed around and slowly descended into the slide/funnel. He was immediately *Shunted* away to Portal Two.

Danielle ran to the other side of the room, this time forgetting all professional decorum. What she saw horrified her more than before. A creature emerged from the narrow side of the funnel. It was no hamster!

It was another hairless, pinkish-red *demon*. Its eyes were glassy—dark and muted. The creature looked at her with a consciousness and intelligence she didn't think possible. It looked at her with abject and utter **horror**.

It then made a sound of profound and complete sadness. It started as a profane, guttural grunt. Ever so slowly the noise turned into a low, mournful gurgling. The cacophony rose slowly, higher and higher, to a shrill and wild wail – a wail so execrably *human* and so consumed by misery it could not possibly belong to any low beast born of this earth.

It was a doleful, dark, dangerous sound. *Unworldly.* Its wretched eyes looked at her, and she could not breathe; she was stricken by terror. The hamster's glassy eyes were watching her, but also not — they were also staring into a frightful *nothingness beyond*.

Its eyes – those, awful wretched eyes! Those eyes carried a depth of knowing that she couldn't fathom. The creature looked *through* her with those eyes, while simultaneously gurgling blood or sputum—she knew not—and then fell over, dead.

Dr. Hastings lost her composure. She screamed. She didn't mean to, but it was an involuntary reaction. She could no more hold it in than she could hold in gasping for air after coming up from being deeply submerged in water.

She ran past the cameras, forgetting to even turn them off or hit pause. She ran upstairs and outside. Nearly doubling over, she panted hard. Her mind and heart raced.

It was still mid-morning. The day was bright and airy. She took deep breaths and tried to regain her composure. She felt suffocated. She felt drained and weakened by a profound sadness she couldn't contemplate or fully understand. She paced around her yard slowly, still gasping for air and occasionally sticking her head towards the sun and closing her eyes—begging the light-giver to provide much-needed warmth. Finally, she caught her breath and stood there—her face basking up the sun, eyes fully closed.

The light on her face did help. After fifteen or twenty minutes of just standing there squeezing her eyes shut and desperately seeking answers to questions she could barely find the words to form, she brought her head down and walked morosely back into the house.

She'd do just one more important test before calling her contact at the US government.

CHAPTER 13

Danielle opened the door with new resolve. This was HER project. She started it. She was going to finish it. She headed downstairs to her basement lab. The familiar buzzing of the Portals was in the air.

Wasting no time, she grabbed a plastic bag and walked over to Portal Two. She did not even look down; she just grabbed the hamster and placed it in the bag using nothing but touch to guide her. Her eyes stayed fixed on the walls. Large globs of matted fur on the creature's pinkish-white skin stuck to her gloves. She just shoved everything in the bag without looking.

Walking back to her computer, Danielle blindly placed the bag containing the *demon* in the desk drawer with the other *demon*. She averted her eyes and didn't dare look. She slammed the drawer shut. She then walked over and grabbed the last hamster from the cardboard box.

The cameras were still rolling from before, so she didn't need to turn them back on. She had lost the heart for all pomp and circumstance—and with it, all attempts at scientific rigor. She was going to try a fresh approach. She removed the jerry-rigged "hamster slide" device she had put together using a funnel and books. Clearing the working area around the *Donut*, she wished to try a new experiment. Taking the hamster by its body, she turned him around—head facing her. She then slowly and carefully pushed the hamster through the portal *butt-first*.

The hamster was kicking and clawing the entire way. She knew from experience when she had *Shunted* part of her fingers several months ago that the feeling was almost electrochemical. She recalled it wasn't painful, but it wasn't entirely pleasant either. Kind of like getting a very gentle shock from a mild electrical current.

The hamster in her hands continued to twitch. She now had placed some of her hand through Portal One—feeling the vibrations in her fingers. All that remained to be seen of the hamster was its head.

She held it there for several moments. She looked it in the eyes, willing it to provide some secrets to the process that devastated her last two trials. It just looked around the room and squirmed uncomfortably. Occasionally one of its paws would break through the portal as she held it there, which created an odd optical illusion of random hamster-hands coming into and out of focus in the middle of the air.

At last, she pulled the entire creature back. She looked it in the eyes. It gazed around the room, its eyes darting to and fro. It looked and behaved perfectly normal.

She looked at its hindquarters. Normal. It was the same brownish-red hamster as always. She put it back in the box. It sniffed around, grabbed a piece of untouched bread still in the corner, and started eating.

This was so strange. She began to speak aloud to herself.

"*The Shunt* effect did not visually or nominally impact

either my hand or the hamster when left in a prolonged state of transference in the Portal. The subject's upper region— its head—remained *un-Shunted* during the duration. As a result, the hamster seemingly has experienced no deleterious effects of any kind."

She mused all this more for herself than for the sake of the cameras. Talking things out loud, alone in her lab, was a familiar pastime at this point in her lonely career. And she needed familiar. She needed something to ground her.

She mused to herself as much as for the cameras, "It's all so very peculiar…"

"Quite peculiar indeed!" a man's gruff voice spoke from the other side of the room.

CHAPTER 14

"What. The. Heck?" Ava's eyes were wide again. "Dad, are you sure this is a true story? You sound like you're making stuff up like usual."

"Oh, no, honey, all quite real. Very thoroughly researched and documented. I wouldn't be a very good scientist if I didn't get my facts straight."

Kayla then noticed the officials clothed in white around the corner getting the last passengers in the neighboring terminal ready for transport. She motioned to her husband with fingers swirling in the air for Sean to speed things up a bit. "We probably have about a half hour until we have to go," she said sweetly.

"Oh, Mum. But I still don't even know the first thing about *the Shunt*. Dad is taking forever! Why do I need to get a shot? He hasn't even explained that yet. And WHAT'S WRONG with the hamsters?"

"Well, let me try to finish up quickly, sweetie. It's all connected, I promise. But before I explain the hamsters and the shots, we have to deal with a little politics—"

****

Danielle screamed! She looked up to see a man in a full suit and tie walk closer to her. He was sandwiched between two large military officers with automatic weapons.

"Don't be alarmed, Doctor," the man said soothingly. "We're with the government."

"What—what's going on?" Danielle asked in a hushed cry. "Who are you? Why are you here?"

"I'm so sorry to alarm you, Doctor," the man spoke genteelly, "my name is Doctor Nelson. I'm with the *Department of Homeland Security*. My office was monitoring the live video recordings on your private network. We are VERY interested in your new data. Or, I should say – the US Government's new data."

Danielle's heart was beginning to calm slightly. In her state, she was almost glad to see another human being. Even if they were from the government.

"I am pretty sure I don't owe you a report until next Friday," she ventured uncomfortably.

"I'm sure you understand that recent events have caused us to expedite an evaluation of your data?" Doctor Nelson was smiling, but it never reached his eyes. "Unless you're running one of the most curious real-time video scams in modern history, I would say you have quite a discovery on your hands."

"Yes, that was my feeling as well," Danielle stood tall, looking the man in the eye. "But this is still *my* experiment."

"Not anymore, I'm afraid."

The man snapped his fingers and around twenty people in lab coats descended her stairs. Many of them brought equipment she had never seen before. Some of the equipment was items she had only read about in recent scientific journals.

Infrared scanning equipment. Sonar. Specto-analysis. Radio transmitters. X-ray assemblies. Y-ray, beta-ray, alpha-ray, and z-wave wireless devices. Plus, so much more it was hard to keep track.

"We have quite a bit of testing to do. Thank you for your contribution to scientific progress, Doctor. But I think we can take it from here!"

Danielle was incredulous, and she didn't even know what to say. What could she say? The government did fund the final research phase of her project. She didn't really know her legal rights at the moment; but more pressing than that – they had *guns*, and she didn't. And the plain truth that those with guns get to make the rules was far older and far more practiced than any trivial matter such as "law." So, she resigned herself to observe from the sidelines silently.

Doctor Nelson walked slowly over to her computer desk and sat down. He then put on a pair of latex gloves. After analyzing the data on her screen for a few minutes, he shouted back to his team. "It appears legit, gentlemen. This matches what we see on our end. Let's get started."

He stood up, smiled perfunctorily at her, and then walked over to the box containing the last, lucky hamster who remained unaffected by *the Shunt*. He grabbed it and picked it up. He walked slowly over to Portal One.

Placing the hamster carefully between his fingers, he slowly moved it butt-first through the portal—just as she had done earlier. Immediately nine men and women in lab coats were on the other side at Portal Two holding video cameras and data pads. They were scribbling away furiously.

"Rear end of subject specimen appears to be agitated and

wiggling," called one of the lab technicians using an aseptic voice.

Doctor Nelson pushed the wriggling creature further into the hole of the *Donut*. Its left and right front paws were barely visible.

The same lab technician at Portal Two bellowed, "1.6-centimeter further protrusion. No change to live animal subject. Appears to continue to struggle in midair. The internal autonomy of the subject can be discernibly seen from the south vantage point of the portal. A fully circular, yet terminated, view of the animal's organs and cardiovascular system appear to be fully visible."

More lab assistants rushed to the scene, taking cameras with 16" lenses with them. They were taking hundreds of photos per second. Danielle couldn't even hear the buzz of her equipment anymore, which was a novel thing to experience in her once-private sanctuary.

"Proceeding with additional protrusion," yelled Doctor Nelson to the other end, pushing the hamster deeper into the portal. He was now using a long pole with a clasp on it to hold the waist of the animal so that he did not need to put his fingers directly inside the Portal. More men with fancy new equipment moved in and began pointing it at the hamster. There were now over fifteen people on the other side of the room.

Shouts rang out from a new lab tech. "No visible change. Subject test animal maintains modality of vigorous movement in its extremities and appears agitated."

To Danielle, this seemed a rather verbose way to explain the hamster was naturally struggling and trying to escape. A very normal reaction to being held in the air through an interdimensional portal.

"Final particle transference commencing," Doctor Nelson shouted to the other side.

He pushed the remaining visible element of the hamster through the portal: its head. The lab assistants instantly became quiet on the other side of the room. Even from here, Daniele could hear the noise. A dismal, tortured, anguished sound emerged from a creature much too sentient to be an ordinary hamster.

It was guttural and anguished beyond all reason. Danielle instinctively looked away from Portal Two and covered her mouth to avoid gasping. However, she suddenly noticed a large 72" monitor had been placed by her computer. On the monitor was a live feed from a high-definition video recording being taken by the lab technicians on the other side of the room.

The live video was zoomed in fully; it was showing the hamster—if it *could* be called a hamster. It was a pealing, cracked, and broken wretch. It looked weathered by time itself. It looked beyond pitiful, deformed by eternal age and boundless sorrow.

And its *EYES* – its damned, glassy, soulless eyes were now meticulously visible with all the savage horrors of 4K. They stared back at the camera with all-knowing, ghastly wonder—with sublime horror and eternal damnable *knowing*. The thing opened its mouth and made that woeful cry again—an eternal and miserable wale that defied all reason.

"Get a microphone on it!" shouted Doctor Nelson, staring at the screen with his mouth hanging open.

The noise from the speakers mixed eerily with a sound that carried across the room from the dark creature itself and blended with the low, electronic pulsating from the portals. The lights flickered.

Black eyes – like a doll's eyes – glassy and stained with blood – stared through an eternal abyss and then at the camera. Its eyes cried out for redemption far worse than the dismal, hellish sound it emanated from its ruined soul. It was a warped and doleful *demon*.

Then it screamed a piercing, hellish scream, fell over, and died.

CHAPTER 15

Of course, Sean didn't explain any of these somber and macabre details to his family. Nor did much of this information ever get out to the public. He only knew any of this due to his mountain of research, including some of the preserved, original video feeds from fifty years ago. The abridged tale he told his family of Doctor Danielle Hastings was one of scientific discovery and unfortunately some dead hamsters.

Of course, the latter vastly outweighed the scientific breakthrough for his dear daughter.

"Dad?"

"Yes, Sweetums."

"WHAT. HAPPENED. TO. THE. HAMSTERS?!?!" Ava was getting more than a little aggravated.

"Well, sweetie. Here's the thing. We don't really know. Not really. We have a lot of guesses. We have a lot of theories. Us 'nerds,' as you call us, have been working on the problem for over fifty years. So, it's not exactly an easy thing to explain. Here's what I can tell you though. As you'll learn in high school, it's called the *Shunt Effect*."

"The *Shunt Effect*? Like the *Shunt Process*?"

"Well, yes and no. Obviously the *Shunt Process* is the science underlying the transformation of particles into energy and then rematerialization of the data-matter stream…"

Mom spoke up quickly, "It's the magic, *Floo Powder* part. It's what beams people to another place, sweetie. That's the *Shunt Process*."

Sean pushed his glasses up past the bridge of his nose, "Yes, yes. Quite so, thank you honey. So, the *Shunt Process* does the heavy lifting. The *Shunt Effect* is the unknown factor that impacts **the mind**. It's how *the Shunt* impacts a living organism's consciousness and mental state."

"The hamsters all died because of their 'mental state?' What does that mean? Daddy, for once in your life, just speak English." Ava was starting to get really mad, and her nostrils flared—just like her mother's when she was upset. Sean knew in a few years he would be hopelessly outmanned.

"Okay, let me try again. So, think of your brain, right. When you get bored—like when you're in your room all alone by yourself—it's because your brain does not have enough stimulation. Meaning it can't work. Your brain needs to constantly WORK to be busy, to be entertained. Make sense so far…?"

"Yes, I think so."

"Okay, so with you alone in your room – you as bored as humanly possible – your brain is *still* doing a million things at once. Perhaps *billions* of things at once. We still don't fully understand the limits of the human mind. Not even close! This is because of something called (get ready for me to be a nerd, I can't help it) – **neural transduction.**"

"Uh-huh." Ava was still folding her arms.

Kayla looked at him with her eyes, pleading with him to use small words. But he was on a roll and couldn't stop now.

"Yes, *neural transduction*. It's just a fancy way to say, 'brain connection.' The brain has millions and billions of connections with your physical body to keep it ALIVE and AWAKE..."

Ava looked mildly interested so Sean patiently continued...

"See, evolution has created these billions of transducers between the brain and everything else you can see, touch, hear, and smell. This is what scientists call *neural transduction theory,* or 'NTT' for short. We are all encased in transducers. Now, since I know you probably don't know what a *transducer* is – did you know there's one right over there?"

Ava looked over as Sean pointed to a microphone into which an LSA attendant was currently making an announcement—the attendant was letting people know their terminal was about to start the pre-*Shunting* process.

"That microphone is a one-way transducer. It's taking a signal, which is just vibrating air, but the vibration has a pattern to it, and it's converting that signal into an electrical signal and that electrical signal has roughly the same pattern. I say *roughly* because it depends on how good the microphone is."

Kayla rolled her eyes and signaled that it was time to hurry this up. The attendant just called their *Shunt* terminal. The Pre-*Shunt* safety checklist was beginning. Sean quickened his explanation.

"But that's what transducers do. They take signals from one medium and send them to another medium. Our bodies, in fact, the bodies of ALL organisms, are *encased* in transducers. Your eye is a transducer; it's taking electromagnetic radiation and it's turning it into what? *Neural signals.* Guess what else? Your ears. They're taking vibrating air and turning it into neural signals. Your nose! It's taking airborne chemicals and turning them into neural signals. Your tongue is taking liquid-borne chemicals and turning them into neural signals. And then the *pièce de résistance* is … your skin. Your skin is an amazing transducer, which does at least three different kinds of things. It can transduce temperature into neural signals, pressure, and texture. You, my dear child, are *head-to-toe* encased in transducers!"

"Okay. So, these trans dozers basically send lots of data and signals to the brain. Got it. This is actually very interesting by the way. I think I'm actually learning something … *Doctor Daddy.*" She giggled.

"It's hard not to be excited. Transduction is the 11th wonder of the world. At least when it comes to autonomy. It connects the conscious brain to the physical world. Your mind can never be truly bored because it's interpreting billions of pieces of information every millisecond."

The government agents were now coming to the top of their aisle. They were starting to hand out safety material. Ava began to notice people recently injected and sleeping in the other aisle and tensed up immediately. Then a question came to her.

"So, how do the shots fit in?"

"Well, that actually took a while to figure out. After the government stepped in and took over Doctor Hasting's experiment, it immediately all became classified! In fact, I'm probably one of maybe a hundred people who even know a lot of this stuff. However, my research allowed me access to some old records from roughly fifty years ago. Before figuring out what was happening, the government, unfortunately, sent

THE SHUNT ✦ SEAN DEMPSEY

many more innocent creatures through *the Shunt* portals to test the device."

Ava grimaced.

"The government soon built portals five times – then ten times – the size of the original. It takes *quite* a bit more power, but the principles are identical. The scientists sent in mice, rats, and even opossums. By the hundreds—if the stories are to be believed. In every single case, the results were the same. Delirium, *madness*, and death!

"Dr. Hastings sadly was no longer leading the experiments at this point. If anything, she was a 'titular head' of the project (at best); in reality, she was *out* for all practical purposes. Otherwise, I believe so many unnecessary animals wouldn't have been sacrificed on the altar of science. Eventually, the good news was that some research assistants finally came up with a brilliant idea. They suggested trying to *Shunt* lab subjects after being put down with a form of anesthesia that shuts down all mental activity. And guess what?"

"It worked?" Ava asked, her eyes wide again.

"It worked. No issue whatsoever. The animals awoke 20 or 30 minutes later, completely unaware of the proceeding and no worse for wear. So, they tried this technique hundreds of times. They did thousands of experiments on live animals over the next few years. They sent in monkeys and rabbits; mice, cats, dogs—and even a 6-ft alligator (I don't have proof of this, but it's a heavily cited anecdote when I did my book's research)."

Kayla caught herself inadvertently laughing at the thought of a room full of scientists wrestling with a live alligator. Ava giggled, too.

"Eventually one brave man named Lucas Williams stepped forward as the first volunteer to *Shunt*. So, on October 3, 2026, the first successful human *Shunt* took place. It happened in Cincinnati, Ohio (in the United States of America). Lucas travelled instantaneously to Washington DC. He was unconscious, of course. But when he awoke, he went through about a million medical tests. He didn't have so much as a case of hiccups. He was perfectly fine.

"However, as is always the case with government, it wasn't all roses and fairy-dust. The *Shunt* has a very dark past. I actually wrote several chapters in my book about it. Here, I can read you a brief excerpt from my manuscript...."

Sean reached for his phone and quickly pulled up his book's first draft. He narrated aloud:

> "Now, if the rumors can be believed – and our research suggests they can – not even six months after Dr. Hasting's initial experiments, some feelers were put out to condemned death-row inmates in Huntsville, Texas, USA. These condemned men were given a chance—a life-or-death chance—'to redeem themselves and become a rare patriot for their country.' The men could either face the electric chair – or take *the Shunt* without anesthesia.
>
> One of the condemned, a man named Robert Crass—whose "number was up," so-to-speak—discussed the matter with his lawyer. Texas being the no-nonsense state that it is, Crass had a less-than-zero chance for parole, and his sentence was to be carried out in a few days. Crass was a triple homicide offender—having murdered three elderly persons while sleeping in their beds at an old folk's home. He was told he could die by electric chair or gain his liberty—even at the risk of him most certainly killing additional victims. He chose *the Shunt*.

The next day he was flown into Boston for the spectacle.

Hundreds of scientists and politicians were present to observe the event. It was highly classified; but our readers will note that it is very tough to keep wraps on truly monumental events, especially ones with such a massive footprint. The story leaked.

Shackled at the hands and feet, Crass was led to *the Shunt* device and ordered to walk through. On just the other side – New York City, freedom, and a full pardon. He just needed to take a few steps.

His knees buckled and beads of sweat peppered his brow; but faced with certain execution and a potential commute of his death sentence, the mind can goad the body into the most frightful actions— even when it's a single step. Crass closed his eyes, took a deep breath, stepped through the Portal, and *Shunted*...

CHAPTER 16

Crass arrived precisely where expected: emerging from the second Portal located approximately 220 miles away in New York City.

However, what walked out of that portal was barely human!

Again, dear readers, please note this information was once highly classified—and we have only disjointed accounts to go on—but apparently what occurred was as follows:

Crass made a single step forward, his eyes glassy and far away. His beard, previously black and full, was now patchy and falling out in clumps. And the hair on his head had gone pure white.

He stared forward, not moving a centimeter. Then he spoke—barely even an audible whisper. "*It's ... it's forever in there.*"

"*Forever...*" his whisper trailed off, as his glassy eyes seemed to be seeing into the void of eternity itself.

He then howled an inhumane *scream!* He moaned like a wild and diseased animal, tearing at his skin and completely biting off his lips and fingers. The correctional officers waiting to receive him shot him in horror until he lay still—

Professor Dempsey stopped reading the manuscript on his phone and looked up at his family.

Kayla was fuming. "Sean! Oh my God! What on earth are you doing reading our girl this nonsense!? And now of all times—right before we *Shunt*. Can you try to bring it around? Maybe self-sensor just a *little*…? Explain that it's all better now. That there are no more issues! That all is going to be fine! That thousands of people *Shunt* every day without a problem. Maybe say something *soothing… Fatherly* even?"

Sean was nonplused and felt more than a little ashamed. "But—I thought…" he stammered, "I thought it was important to explain the history and the risk involved. She's almost thirteen, Kay. She can handle it." He nearly said that actually he HAD been censoring himself quite a bit.

Kayla stood up and reached out her hand for her daughter to take it. Ava stood up next to her.

"Let's go for a quick walk, Cake. Maybe you and I can get some ice cream. Let Dad think about what he's done…"

Ava looked deeply at her father and was surprisingly calm and serene – almost introspective. But the thought of ice cream knocked her out of her reverie. She took her mother's hand, and they sauntered over to an overpriced cart doling out frozen treats.

I was self-censoring! Sean thought angrily. *A lot.*

For example, he didn't mention anything about any of the legal cases – *two entire chapters* worth in his book – where *the Shunt* was used to torture and *murder* people. So many more cases than he thought would exist. It was mind-bending—the brutality of mankind. He didn't say a thing about that!

For example, he didn't breathe a word about the case of Dr. Cathleen Rogers, who forty-two years ago had caught her husband in bed, brazenly cheating on her with a far younger woman.

She cried for an entire night, then talked with her husband the next day about 'looking past the incident' and moving on together. He was repentant and she swore him to future fidelity. She tearfully took him back.

Nevertheless, just two weeks later, she snuck her husband past the security desk at her office in Washington DC. As later admitted in court, she lured him there under false pretenses to show him *the Shunt* device—the discovery she'd been diligently working on for the past year in the government's lab.

Dr Rogers fired up *the Shunt* while giving her unsuspecting husband a tour. At this point, *Shunt* units were all the standard 3x3 meters and buzzed loudly with electricity like a small power plant. The rest of the story was chronicled via heavily-redacted security tapes. Sean had just watched the footage last week. It was *extremely fresh* in his mind. He sat back in his seat and recalled it in detail…

****

"I wanted to show you why I've been so absent. I—I again just want to apologize," Cathleen nearly yelled to her husband over the booming electric currents in the room as she walked down the metal staircase to her lab.

He descended the staircase alongside her and looked

around in a fascinated way. This stuff was state-of-the-art. Probably millions of dollars of tech in here. It was incredible! "Honey, it's okay. We're over this. We've talked it through. What's done is done. Forgotten. We have turned over a new leaf. I've changed. You've changed. It's all in the past."

The man smiled at his wife. Doctor Rogers looked at her husband oddly for a moment. Then she raised her voice above the din, "This equipment, behind you, has been my responsibility and the focus of the research. It's incredible, isn't it?"

"I think I read about this in Time *magazine. Does it really live up to all the recent hype? Do you feel this thing can actually end the energy crisis?"*

*"It can do all that **and more**, darling. Let me show you." She pressed a button on the computer and the buzzing intensified; the portal turned from see-through to a very thin opaque shade of gray. "Check this out – here, look at the shimmering wave of the—"*

The man turned to gaze at the portal, almost touching it. At that moment, Dr. Rogers lunged forward and PUSHED her husband into the portal with all her might. He disappeared immediately and was Shunted. *She then sauntered over to the computer terminal, whistling. She pressed a button, and the humming subsided. "See you in hell, babe." She laughed a wicked laugh.*

****

The security footage had given Sean vivid nightmares for almost four days straight.

He also knew the trial that followed; he had reviewed all the evidence and legal transcripts. This, too, fascinated him. For no case had ever existed quite like it; there was no established precedent for such a crime before *The State v. Rogers*.

Dr. Rogers had turned off the computer's uplink into *the Shunt* device shortly after pushing her husband. So, as her legal defense argued, she did not actually *murder* anyone. Her husband was still IN there. In *the Shunt* network – somewhere, lost. Un-constituted particles and raw consciousness. Lost forever. Eternal nothingness, but still always conscious, for all time.

But, as the State argued, yes – he was alive. But he was now reduced to eternal damnation. As the closing arguments went, *"Poor Mr. Rogers is most undoubtedly screaming forever and without sound nor body—without voice—forever and ever and ever. It is a fate far worse than death, ladies and gentlemen. I am sure he prays for death and will throughout ceaseless, restless eternity."*

The jury convicted her on all counts.

His wife and daughter were coming back. Ava had a nice big bowl of chocolate ice cream with a sugar cone on top. His wife looked slightly less upset but still scowling. She was eating a strawberry ice cream on a waffle cone. It wasn't possible to be completely furious with someone while eating strawberry ice cream, he reasoned to himself.

"How much did that cost?" was all he could think of saying. It was stupid. He silently kicked himself.

Kayla's scowl turned into a glare before he could blink twice.

"Okay, Dad. So, I just got to know. I've been thinking." Ava took a lick of ice cream as she pondered, "So, why the dead hamsters? Can you just explain that? I still don't get how *tranzy-duzers* or particle synthesis or government computers or anything would cause the hamsters and bad people to die!"

"Okay, so that's again … still a mystery. But the working theory we have is this—and it's primarily based on the last and final words of our murderous friend Robert Crass…

"He said '*It's **eternity** in there*,' remember? Well, that's our clue! Think again about the human mind. Your mind is doing a billion things – calculations – each and every second. Maybe it's *trillions* each second; we don't really know for sure. Synapses are firing. Emotions are being processed. Itches are seeking to be scratched. Memories are constantly surfacing and being re-buried—such as your over-due algebra homework or a cute boy at school. Plans are being made. Every thought and sensation is packaged and processed—plus, a million other things related to movement, smell, taste, and feeling.

"Now think for a second about what would happen if for some reason your mind couldn't connect or *interface* with the rest of your senses – if your consciousness became DETACHED for even a split moment in time. Well, then your mind – the part that makes you **YOU** – would experience a virtual *eternity*. Eternal and endless time! Eternal boredom without sensory perception or bodily connection…

"Think of it this way. Your conscious mind would live a million-billion years of NOTHINGNESS. Your thinking self – your *soul,* for lack of a better word – would have *nothing* to do with its millions of neuro connectors. Your conscious mind would literally bore itself to death. You would live virtually *forever* in the blink of an eye and never have any substance – any feeling. No touch, no sight, no senses of any kind. You would just **BE** – endless and eternal. Forever and ever and ever and ever.

"Billions upon billions upon billions of years. Eons of ceaseless consciousness living in a single all-encompassing moment!

"In short, it would drive a person to utter madness. Complete and total madness. That is what the *Shunt Effect* is. That is what killed the hamsters."

CHAPTER 17

Ava stared at her shoes. Kayla was quiet too. It was a lot to take in.

His wife cleared her voice and broke the silence. "I preferred the other way you put it in one of the final sections of your book, which you asked me to review the other night. How the unconnected mind loses its ability to tap into the universe, or something?"

Sean smiled. "Ah, thank you for remembering, darling. You've always been the biggest fan of my work, you know." He hoped he was getting brownie points for sucking up. "Well, yes, I think that's probably a better, albeit less scientific, way to explain it."

Ava smiled, "That sounds more like my kind of explanation!"

Sean frowned, "Well, think of it this way. Remember those transducers I mentioned earlier – the connections between your brain and physical body? Well, there are mysteries of the human mind that even science can't yet unravel. For example, some new theories suggest that there is an *unknown* transducer

– likely formed through millions of years of evolution, mind you – but some unknown transducer that somehow connects the conscious mind with the fabric of the universe itself. Or said another way – it connects one's *Soul* to *God*! When that transducer is impaired or severed, albeit for even an infinitesimal amount of time, the Soul's connection with a higher purpose or *higher consciousness* is lost forever. The mind becomes disconnected for all time! Some religions might even refer to that as 'Hell' or *eternal damnation…*"

Ava stared forward and bit her lip. Soupy, melting ice cream sat untouched in her bowl.

Sensing the gravity of his words and their almost apocryphal nature for a scientist such as himself, Sean felt it was time to turn a corner in the conversation.

"But it's all good, sweetie. See, just like any dangerous tool, knowing how to work with it is crucial. For example, you'd never think of operating a chainsaw without ear plugs and eyewear, right?"

Attempting to explain a chainsaw to a 12-year-old girl probably wasn't the best approach. He tried again.

"Or, eh—I mean, you'd never want to go on a rollercoaster without being strapped in. The seatbelts protect you from flying out. It's the same thing with *the Shunt*. The injection keeps you safe. It stops your conscious mind from getting disconnected. It makes everything super *safe*!"

He smiled as lovingly as he knew, "*The Shunt* is super safe, sweet pea. There have been thousands of *Shunts* a day for the last forty or fifty years. *The Shunt* saved humanity! It's perhaps the greatest scientific invention of all time. It's a very powerful, yet dangerous tool; so, it's important to listen to the LSA technicians when they come around."

His timing couldn't have been better. Three LSA attendants were just entering their row with a metal cart. They wheeled it down the line and began talking to the passengers next to them.

"But *Daddy*. I'm still scared." Ava looked at her feet again, almost trembling. "But – I'm not scared of eternal life or anything. That actually sounds kinda fun. I just don't want to get *a shot*. I hate shots! You know what happened at the dentist last year. I'm a sissy. You just need to accept your daughter is a complete sissy. I'm sorry."

Sean felt his temper flaring but then stopped himself. "Sweetie, you just don't understand. Mankind can't stare into an empty abyss. *Man wasn't designed to glimpse eternity.* Maybe if I had more time to explain—but … it's too late now. It's time to go. Please just listen to your parents. Trust us on this!"

A tall woman donned in white was standing in front of them, "Hi, everyone. I'll be your *Shunting* administrator today. Do we have any 'first-timers' here?" The government official was overly cheery and bright. However, she was flanked by two less-than-chipper attendants whose dopey and listless expressions didn't change.

Sean addressed her, "Yes, hi. Thanks so much. No, for me; but my family here will be *Shunting* for the first time."

The nameless female LSA official was filling out paperwork and barely looking at him as she spoke.

"Wonderful, just *wonderful!*" She spoke in sanguine tones of airy delight. Sean didn't know how she kept it up with each passenger. She finally looked down from her clipboard at the 12-year-old staring up at her. "And who do I have the pleasure of meeting today?"

"Ava," she replied quietly.

"Ava! Such a beautiful name. Ava, yes, here you are. I have you down for a single dose of *Propofol*. Can you verify?"

Ava spoke up with quiet resolve, "No shot for me today, please."

Sean almost lost his mind. "*NO!* I mean -- YES, yes, that's quite *CORRECT*. She'll be taking an injection of Propofol today. Thank you very much, miss."

The woman looked flustered and turned back to Ava, "Ava, I need you to say you agree. Can you say you understand for me?"

"I understand. And I do NOT agree. What are the other options, please?"

"Ava—by Heaven or Hell, if I need to strap you down to force your injection in you myself, I swear to God I will!" Professor Dempsey seethed.

"*Doctor Daddy*, please. Chill, dude. I'm addressing my assigned *Shunting Attendant* right now. We are discussing my private, personal medical options if you don't mind?"

Her father almost lost it. But somehow, he kept it together. Luckily the nameless attendant spoke instead.

"Uh, eh—well, yes. Well, legally I need all *Shunt* passengers to verbally consent to the medical procedure. I see you've been studying our literature." She motioned to the pamphlet in Ava's left hand. Sean hadn't even noticed his daughter holding it earlier. "Yes, there is the option of anesthesia gas for any passengers who refuses, or cannot take, the injection."

Ava spoke up in the most professional tone she could muster, "Yes, ma'am. I believe I will choose that option if you please. I would most prefer to side-step any unnecessary jabs today if they can be avoided."

Although livid, Sean almost smiled. His daughter was doing a *bad impression* of him. Her tone oozed sarcasm, but he couldn't help but feel slightly amused by how well she handled herself. She had grown up so fast! He still thought of her as his young baby girl, scared to go to bed without ten different nightlights turned on. Back then it always looked like an ancient airport runway in her bedroom at night. Now she was holding her own with government officials! *Time is a cruel villain*, he wistfully thought to himself.

"And you're sure it's still a *hundred percent* trustworthy, ma'am?" asked Kayla to the attendant.

"Oh, yes, absolutely, miss. Before the 2060s, anesthesia was the primary method of pre-*Shunt* administration. It's perfectly safe, just not as often requested. But I can go retrieve a gas mask and tank now. I'll be right back."

"And there's no extra cost for this, right???" spoke up Sean, imploringly.

But the attendant had already turned around and was bringing her entourage of two mindless helpers with her. She didn't hear him – or at least pretended not to.

"Ava, I swear to God—"

"Dad, don't worry. I've been reading this government brochure. It says right here: '*There are numerous* safe and effective *alternatives for inducing pre-*Shunt *unconsciousness. Please see your* Shunt *attendant for more information.*' See, it's all in the fine print."

"She's her father's daughter!" Kayla spoke up. She seemed to be somehow enjoying the repertoire.

"Fine. Just fine. But **please** just behave so we can get to New Guinea as fast as possible."

His cheeky little girl winked at him. She was growing up.

Making her own decisions. Forming her own opinions.

He didn't know if he liked it!

The metal cart came back after a few minutes. It was a different nameless attendant pushing it—a bald man wearing the same sterile, white uniform. A honeysuckle and administrative voice came over the loudspeaker as it approached, "Shunt Terminal #16. *Three minutes* until group-*Shunt*. Three minutes. Please take your final injections now. This is your **final** warning prior to *Shunting*."

The woman in white with the overly rosy disposition was nowhere to be seen. On the cart was a small gas mask and a large tank was hanging off the side.

"Seats 112, 113, and 114? You ready?" the bald man pushing the cart seemed almost bored. He had the energy of a carsick basset hound. But at this point in the commute, Sean was exhausted and barely cared. He was ready to get to New Guinea.

"Ready, here," he replied. "See you on the other side, family. It's going to be a vacation to remember!"

The bald man in white grabbed a pair of latex gloves and slid them on. He reached for one of a hundred pre-filled syringes from a plastic basket hidden within the cart behind a cloth overhang. He yanked off the stopper at the end of the needle and approached Professor Dempsey.

"One, two, three. Here we go." He stuck the needle in his arm and pushed in the liquid.

"See you soon, darlings…" was the last thing Sean said dopily before passing out.

CHAPTER 18

S ean awoke groggily. He didn't know the time or how long he was out. But his location certainly had changed. He was now lying on his back, staring at a bright, white ceiling. It was far warmer, too. He looked over; his wife was wheeling in next to him now. She was still unconscious.

He looked down at the bottom of the moving chair as it came to a gentle stop. He had never seen the chairs in motion before; in all his prior *Shunts* he just had woken up and then proceeded on his way. His mind was already abuzz with scientific curiosity about the equipment.

The chairs moved along what seemed to be an invisible conveyor belt—but were not visibly connected to any moving parts. It was all frictionless, and they navigated by simple programming and likely some sort of hover technology he hadn't yet studied.

The chair lifted his wife up by three or four feet, then folded back, splaying her out horizontally as if on a bed.

"Honey, honey," he said gingerly. She looked like she was stirring.

"You okay? All good?" She opened her eyes and seemed confused. Then she looked panicked. "Ava! Oh Ava, where is she?"

"What? What do you mean?"

"Right after you went under, the attendants seemed really confused about the proper dosage of anesthesia. They were arguing with each other. I then was stabbed and lost consciousness."

"Oh, it'll be fine, Sweetie. The government does this sort of thing all the time. She'll be along shortly."

Sure enough, a third chair started slowly wheeling into the room. On it was their daught---

No!

Seat-belted into the chair stared a *thing*. Unmoving, it gazed forward, wide awake! Eyes like hazy orbs.

A monstrously aged and deformed creature.

The *thing* slowly wheeled forward on the conveyor belt and time seemed to stand still. Its hair was completely ashen-white and falling out in clumps by its forehead.

Its *eyes* – its damned *eyes* – were open: wide, **wide open**. Staring, staring. Staring into complete nothingness.

Glassy. Blank. Dull. *Lifeless eyes.*

Vacant eyes!

Eyes that appeared to have seen timeless eternity and endless sorrow over and over and over again.

The creature --- the *thing* that was their daughter – it turned to them. But its eyes never moved.

"Longer than you think..." it muttered with madness. "Longer than you think, Daddy! ... I saw. I saw! Dear God, I saw!"

Kayla grabbed Sean's arm with both hands and was paralyzed. She squeezed hard, cutting off his circulation. Neither of them dared to breathe. They stared in abject horror and were utterly paralyzed

"I *saw*, Daddy! I saw. So much longer than you think, Daddy." The creature's voice was rising above a muted whisper.

"**Longggg** *Shunt*, Daddy. Real long. Long *Shunt*. Longer than you can think, Daddy."

It grew agitated and began to writhe and contort its body. The thing on the seat bit off its tongue and then began to claw madly at its eyeballs.

With chalky white talons, it ripped out both its eyes and threw them to the ground. Blood splattered everywhere and was gushing onto the floor and all over the white seats and white carpet.

"*Longer than you can think, Doctor Daddy,*" came a dark, hellish, guttural voice – it was monotone, inhuman.

Attendants were rushing in now. A deafening alarm was going off and glaring, red lights were flashing. His wife was sobbing uncontrollably and screaming at the top of her lungs. "*My baby! My baby!!*" she howled. "*LOOK WHAT YOU BASTARDS HAVE DONE TO MY BABY!*"

The *thing* gurgled and laughed in a wild and profane way— as more *Shunt* attendants flooded the room and began wheeling it away. The creature just continued to claw mercilessly at its bloody, empty eye sockets – at eyes that had seen into a nameless and unseeable *void* forever and ever and ever.

The body of the creature convulsed violently. While it writhed and spasmed, it cackled things in a hysterical and sunken madness, and then began to scream. Shrill, excruciating, lugubrious screams bounced madly off the walls and reverberated in all their ears.

But Professor Dempsey didn't hear anything more because by then he had fallen to his knees and was screaming too.

ABOUT THE AUTHOR

SEAN DEMPSEY

I am a husband, a father, an entrepreneur, a son,
a poet, a friend, and – occasionally—an author.

.

I began this novella on a whim—in a vain attempt to improve
my writing skills. Horror is hardly my genre, but with fresh
challenges come new horizons.

It was a risky endeavor, and I imagine this work will be
derided as not only derivative, but woefully executed as well.
However, as a far wise man than I once said:

"To win without risk is to triumph without glory."
   - Pierre Corneill

Printed in Great Britain
by Amazon

63327569R00057